P9-DFU-974

Ex-Library: Friends of
Lake County Public Library

THREE LITTLE PIGS AND
THE BIG BAD WOLF

written and illustrated by GLEN ROUNDS

Holiday House / New York

LAKE COUNTY PUBLIC LIBRARY

3 3113 01221 1860

Copyright © 1992 by Glen Rounds
Printed in the United States of America
All rights reserved
First Edition

Library of Congress Cataloging-in-Publication Data
Rounds, Glen, 1906–
    Three little pigs and the big bad wolf / written and illustrated
  by Glen Rounds.
            p.   cm.
    Summary: Relates the adventures of three little pigs who leave
  home to seek their fortunes and how they deal with the big bad wolf.
    ISBN 0-8234-0923-6
    [1. Folklore. 2. Pigs—Folklore.]
  PZ8.1.R77TH   1992   91-18173   CIP   AC
  398.2—dc20
  [E]

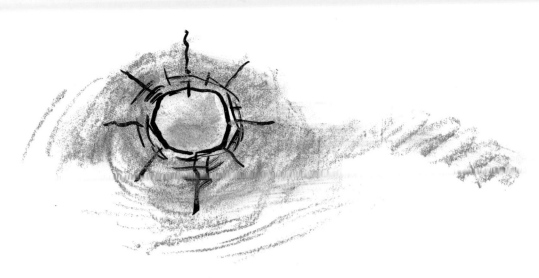

For my wife, Elizabeth High

One morning a long time ago an old sow called her three little pigs to her and said, "I have something to tell you."

"I love you all very much," she went on, "but you are now big enough to go out into the world and make homes for yourselves."

So that very day, the three little pigs said good-bye to the old sow and set off down the road.

"Build yourselves good, strong homes," the old sow called after them, "AND WATCH OUT FOR THE BIG BAD WOLF."

They hadn't gone far when the first little pig saw a pile of STRAW in a nearby field.

"I can build a cozy house inside that pile of STRAW!" he cried. "And THE BIG BAD WOLF will never find me!"

So, while he started building his house, the other two little pigs went on down the road.

A little while later, when they were passing a big pile of STICKS, the second little pig said, "I can use those STICKS to build a house so strong THE BIG BAD WOLF could *never* get inside!"

So the third little pig went on down the road alone.

He had gone quite a way, across a bridge, past a turnip patch, and around a bend, when he saw a tiny BRICK house that nobody had lived in for a long time.

It had a good strong door, and when the little pig went inside, he found there was even a fireplace and a big black kettle on the hearth.

"THE BIG BAD WOLF could never get into this BRICK house!" he said to himself, so he shut the door and made himself at home.

For a long time the three little pigs lived safely in their new houses.

Then one day THE BIG BAD WOLF came to the first little pig's STRAW house.

He scratched on the door and called out, "Little pig! Little pig! Let me come in!"

"NO! NO!" cried the little pig. "By the hairs on my CHINNY-CHIN-CHIN, I'll *not* let you in!"

"Then," growled the wolf, "I'll HUFF and I'll PUFF and I'll BLOW your house in!"

AND THAT'S JUST WHAT HE DID!

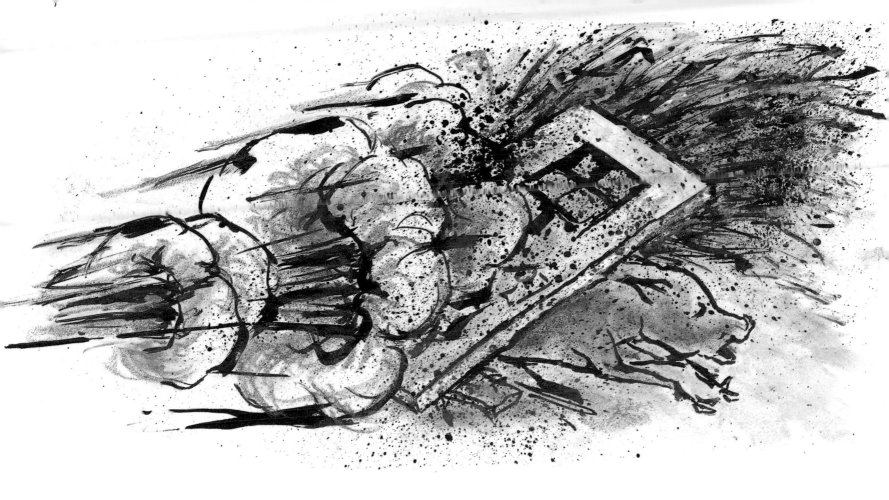

He HUFFED and he PUFFED and he BLEW the little pig's house in.

AND THEN HE
ATE THE LITTLE PIG!

On another day the second little pig, inside the house built of STICKS, heard THE BIG BAD WOLF outside saying, "Little pig! Little pig! Let me come in!"

"No! No!" cried the little pig. "By the hairs on my CHINNY-CHIN-CHIN, I'll *not* let you in!"

"Then," said the wolf, "I'll HUFF and I'll PUFF and I'll BLOW your house in!"

AND THAT'S JUST WHAT HE DID!

He HUFFED and he PUFFED and he BLEW the little pig's house in.

AND THEN HE ATE THAT LITTLE PIG!

A few days later, the third little pig looked out his window and saw THE BIG BAD WOLF looking in.

"Little pig! Little pig!" said the wolf, "Let me come in!"

"No! No!" cried the little pig, "not by the hairs on my CHINNY-CHIN-CHIN, I'll *not* let you in!"

"Then," snarled the wolf, "I'll HUFF and I'll PUFF and I'll BLOW your house in!"

And that's just what he *tried* to do!

He HUFFED and he PUFFED!
And he PUFFED and he HUFFED!

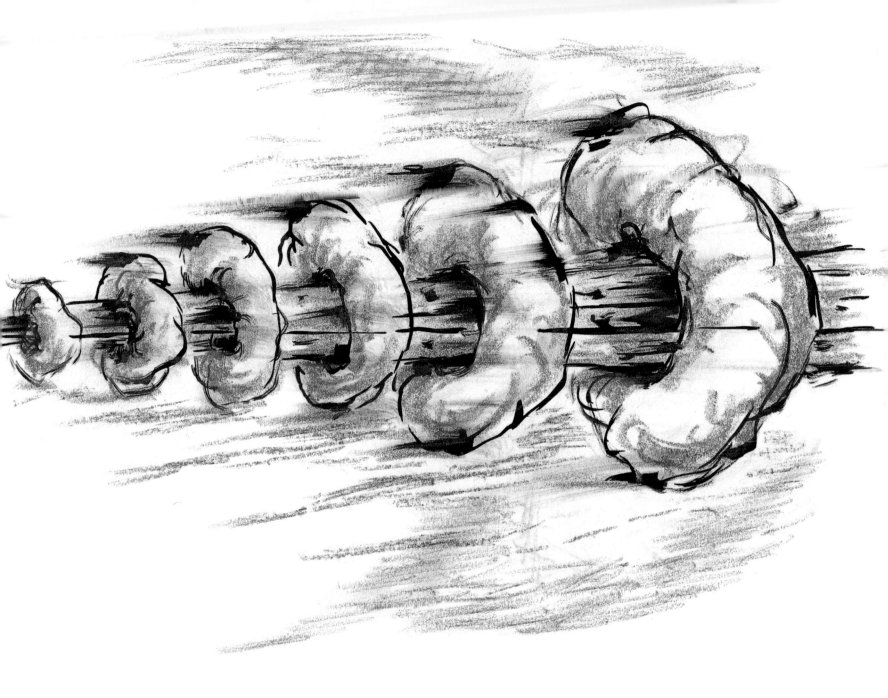

But no matter how hard he HUFFED and PUFFED, he couldn't blow the little BRICK house in!

Now **THE BIG BAD WOLF** was very angry when he found that he couldn't BLOW the little pig's house down.

But he put on a big smile and called out, "Little pig! Little pig! I know where there's a field of the sweetest turnips you'll ever taste. I'll come by tomorrow morning at SIX o'clock to show you where they are!"

"I'll be ready," the little pig answered from inside his house.

But the little pig already knew where the turnip patch was, so he went there by himself at FIVE o'clock.

When **THE BIG BAD WOLF** came by at SIX o'clock to pick him up, the third little pig was safe inside his house again.

The wolf scratched on his door and called, "Little pig! Little pig! Are you ready?"

The little pig looked out the window and cried, "You are late! I've already been to the field and gotten a nice basket of turnips!"

THE BIG BAD WOLF was VERY, VERY ANGRY when he found that the little pig had tricked him!

But in his sweetest voice he called out, "Little pig! Little pig! There's going to be a fair up on the hill this afternoon. I'll come by for you at THREE o'clock and we'll go together."

"Fine!" cried the little pig, "I'll be ready!"

The little pig knew what the wolf had in mind, so he went up the hill early, and had a good time at the fair by himself.

But just as he was starting home, he saw THE BIG BAD WOLF coming up the road, so he jumped into an empty barrel to hide.

The barrel tipped over, and with the little pig inside, went rolling and bouncing down the hill, straight for the wolf.

The wolf was so frightened by the strange sight that he ran off through the woods as fast as he could go!

So the little pig got home safely. He had just put on a big pot of soup to boil, when he heard THE BIG BAD WOLF outside.

"Little pig! Little pig!" the wolf called, "are you ready to go to the fair?"

"I've already been to the fair," the little pig answered. "I was in that barrel that frightened you so much."

When THE BIG BAD WOLF heard that, he was so angry, he jumped onto the roof of the little pig's house and shouted, "I'M TIRED OF YOUR TRICKS, AND

NOW I'M COMING DOWN THE CHIMNEY, AND I'M
GOING TO EAT YOU UP!!!"

But when THE BIG BAD WOLF came down the chimney, he fell headfirst into the big pot of boiling soup!

And that night the little pig had THE BIG BAD WOLF for supper.

And as far as anyone knows, that little pig is still living in his little BRICK house.